W9-ARH-598

The Grumpy Bunny's ™
FIELD TRIP

by Justine Korman

illustrated by Lucinda McQueen

Troll

For Ron, who makes every trip exciting
—J.K.

For Justine, storyteller extraordinaire,
with countless bunny thanks
—Lucinda

This edition published in 2001.

Text copyright © 1998 by Justine Korman.
Illustrations copyright © 1998 by Lucinda McQueen.

Published by WhistleStop, an imprint and registered trademark
of Troll Communications L.L.C.

Grumpy Bunny is a trademark of Justine Korman, Lucinda McQueen,
and Troll Communications L.L.C.

All rights reserved. No part of this book may be reproduced or utilized in any form
or by any means, electronic or mechanical, including photocopying,
recording, or by any information storage and retrieval system, without
written permission from the publisher.

Printed in the United States of America.
ISBN 0-8167-4527-7

10   9   8   7   6   5   4   3   2

The sun was shining brightly the morning of the kinderbunny class field trip. Ten excited kinderbunnies hippety-hopped in front of Easter Bunny Elementary School.

Everyone was smiling—except, of course, the grumpy bunny. This year Hopper was leading the field trip for the first time.

"What if I lose a bunny?" Hopper worried. "What if some bunny gets sick on the bus?"

He tried to count the kinderbunnies as they bounced here, there, and everywhere. "One bunny, two bunnies, three bunnies, four . . . now I need to find six more," the grumpy bunny grumbled.

At last, Hopper had
all ten kinderbunnies
counted.

1, 2, 3, 4, 5, 6, 7, 8, 9, 10

bunnies climbed the steep stairs of the bus.

Hopper had hoped the kinderbunnies would sit still, but they were much too excited. In fact, some of the bunnies bounced right off their bus seats!

The bus ride to the big city was a teacher's nightmare. Hopper tried to calm the riot. But the minute he got one kinderbunny settled down, nine more needed his attention. The grumpy bunny was so distracted, he could barely keep his eyes on the road.

Hopper wasn't the only one who wanted the bus trip to end. Peter couldn't wait to see the dinobunnies. He tugged at Hopper's sleeve. "Are we there yet?"

The grumpy bunny rolled his eyes. "We haven't gone a mile since the last time you asked!"

Finally, the bus arrived at the big museum. Hopper carefully counted the ten kinderbunnies as they left the bus:

1, 2, 3, 4, 5, 6, 7, 8, 9, 10.

BUNNIES OLD

BUNNIES BOLD

Then he counted them again inside the huge museum. Peter's voice echoed through the great hall. "Are we there yet?"

Hopper sighed. "Yes, we are. Now, I want everyone to listen up! Remember the most important rule: Stay together! I don't want any of you wandering off."

The kinderbunnies nodded. "We promise," they said.

BUNNIES
LIVING IN THE COLD

"All right. Let's start with the prehistoric rabbits,"
Hopper decided.

Peter cheered. "Yea! Yea!"

"Sshhh!" Hopper hissed. "A museum is a place for quiet."
He led the bunnies through the arch labeled BUNNIES OLD.

Suddenly, a huge skeleton towered above them! "Bunnysaurus Rex!" Peter whispered in awe.

Hopper's jaw dropped. "That creature looks wilder than a kinderbunny!" he said to himself.

Hopper showed his class the bones of other critters who lived long ago.

"Amazing! I wish we could stay for a week!" Peter squealed.

"I know," Hopper agreed. "But there's so much more to see. Let's move on!"

Peter did not hear Hopper. He was too busy pretending to be a Bunnysaurus Rex.

Next, the kinderbunnies went through the arch marked
BUNNIES BOLD. There they saw shining suits of armor, bright
banners, and sharp swords.

"This is how bunnies fought their battles in the Middle
Ages," Hopper explained.

Daisy and Flopsy were not listening. They were fighting their own battle—over Flopsy's lunch!

The two battling bunnies were left behind when the class moved on to BUNNIES LIVING IN THE COLD.

"Brrr!" Hopper shivered. Just looking at the snowy scenes in the glass cases gave him the chills.

"These bunnies build their homes out of ice and snow," he told the group.

"I wonder what it would be like to be an Eskibunny," mused a dreamy bunny named Dean. He pictured building his very own ice castle and riding a pet seal named Sam.

Dean was far away when Hopper said, "Time for lunch. Follow me!"

The bunnies got out their brown bags. They bought milk and juice—and carrot cake, of course. And they did their usual amount of spilling.While Hopper mopped up, Bingo climbed into the fountain. The class clown couldn't resist striking a funny pose!

In fact, Bingo was having so much fun posing, he didn't see the class move on to the Hall of Art.

The kinderbunnies chased each other past great
masterpieces. Hopper huffed and puffed behind them.
"Wait!" he panted. "You're . . . missing the . . . art!"

But one bunny wasn't missing anything. Arthur
decided to stay and sketch what he saw.

"That's the last stop on our tour," Hopper said. "Line up for the bus, please."

Then he counted: "One, two, three, four . . . there must be six bunnies more!" The grumpy bunny pulled his ears in distress. Where were the other bunnies?

"Oh, no!" Hopper wailed. He wanted to turn the museum upside down to search for his students. "But I'm only one bunny!" he said in despair.

Suddenly, Hopper remembered something his teacher had taught him a long time ago: Think first.

So Hopper sat down and thought.

He thought about each place the bunnies had visited in the museum. He tried to remember where each kinderbunny had been. "I've got it!" Hopper jumped to his feet. "I'll retrace our steps."

Just then the lost bunnies came running to join the group.

"We heard you say, 'Oh, no!'" Peter exclaimed. "Is something wrong?"

Hopper counted his kinderbunnies one through ten and sighed with relief. "Not anymore! Let's go home before anything else can happen."

Quickly Hopper helped the bunnies back on the bus.

Then he sank gratefully into his seat. "What a field trip! This has to be my worst day ever!" the grumpy bunny muttered. "The minute we get back, I'm telling Sir Byron, 'No more field trips for this teacher—never, ever!' I'll put my paw down!"

But a strange thing happened when the bus reached the school. Hopper found himself surrounded by happy kinderbunnies.

"This was the best field trip ever!" Peter declared.

"It was the most fun I've ever had!" Daisy cried.
"No, it was the most fun *I've* ever had!" Flopsy shouted.
And the battling bunnies were at it again, until Sir
Byron appeared.

The Great Hare clapped Hopper on the back and said, "Good job. I'm counting on you to lead the trip again next year."

The grumpy bunny thought about saying no. Then he looked at the giggling kinderbunnies and couldn't remember what he'd been so grumpy about. In fact, Hopper turned to Sir Byron and asked, "Do we have to wait a whole year?"

The best part about traveling
is when the trip is done:
Your eyes are filled with new sights,
and your heart is filled with fun!